Little Tang

Sally Grindley

John Butler

ORCHARD BOOKS

High up in the treetops of the tropical rainforest,
Little Tang held on tightly to his mother. Kara
was devoted to her bright-eyed bundle of
orange fur. She fed him and nursed him,
kept him clean and carried him
everywhere. At night, she
built a nest and curled
herself round him.
Little Tang felt
warm and safe.

By the time he was three years old, Little Tang loved to scamper wildly along branches and swing through the trees, but he often asked Kara to carry him. He could feed himself and played at making nests, but he still suckled his mother and took food from her mouth. Kara was always there, ready to give Little Tang what he wanted.

But now Little Tang was seven years old. Kara knew he was
old enough to learn to look after himself. Soon he would have
to live on his own like other male orangutans and Kara needed
to show him how.

One day, Little Tang wanted to snuggle up to his mother but
she wouldn't let him. Little Tang didn't understand. He hung
from a branch squealing crossly and kicking his legs in the air.

Kara moved to a tree close by to nurse Kinti, Little Tang's baby sister. When Kara picked some fruit and put it in her mouth, Little Tang rushed over and demanded his share. Kara wouldn't give him any. She knew it was important for him to learn to find food for himself.

But Little Tang didn't want to. He put his hands round Kara's cheeks and tried to open her mouth. She hooted crossly and moved to a higher branch.

Little Tang howled in protest. He broke off branches
and hurled them into the air. Then he pushed at
a dead tree and watched it crash to the forest floor.
Why did his mother not want him?

Suddenly another young male orangutan leapt towards him. Little Tang squealed and ran away. The other male caught up with him and tugged at his arm. Little Tang saw that he wanted to play and smacked him in fun. Soon they were wrestling and racing through the treetops together.

Then Little Tang's playmate pulled down some fruit and ate it. Little Tang grabbed some for himself and they sat side by side munching happily.

As it grew dark, Little Tang left his new friend and went back to his mother. He crept into her nest and snuggled up to her. Kara let him stay.

But the next morning he woke up and found she had gone. She was sitting with Kinti on a branch nearby. As Little Tang approached her she moved away. Little Tang hurled himself through the treetops, shrieking with fury.

Day after day the same thing happened. Kara wanted to
be kind, but sometimes she had to be cruel. She allowed
Little Tang into her nest for a while, then she moved out.
She let him play-fight with Kinti, then they rushed away and
left Little Tang on his own. She wanted him to go exploring
without her. He always threw a tantrum, but little by little he
started to enjoy going off by himself.

Soon Little Tang began to leave his mother for longer. He travelled further away to search for his favourite fruits. He learned to build his own day nests and dozed peacefully. But when night fell, he still went back to Kara and slept in her nest.

But one morning, Little Tang woke to see Kara sucking happily at a durian fruit. Little Tang loved durian fruit and squealed at his mother to give him some. Then he tried to snatch it and it dropped to the forest floor. Kara hooted furiously. Little Tang ignored her and peered down through the branches.

Then he did something he had never done before. He launched himself down through the trees and jumped onto the ground. He began to search frantically for the durian fruit.

Suddenly Kara squealed loudly, but Little Tang was too busy to notice her warning. Behind him, a tiger crept slowly forward. Kara screamed again. Little Tang found the durian fruit and leapt up into the trees, just as the tiger pounced and scratched his leg.

Little Tang squealed with pain and ran to Kara for comfort. She kissed his wound clean and fed him with fruit. Later, when it began to rain, she broke off a large leaf and held it over him to keep him dry. Little Tang enjoyed being mothered again and whimpered quietly as he nestled up to her.

But, that night, for the first time, Little Tang built his own nest.
Kara settled down close by, still watching over him.

   Little Tang was sleeping soundly next morning when Kara
went off for the day with Kinti. When he woke, Little Tang
found some food and met up with another young male.
They romped and wrestled for a while,
then set off through the
treetops to find new
fruit trees to raid.

As days passed, Little Tang still spent time with his mother, but more and more often he went off with his playmates or travelled on his own. He found his own food and he built his own nests. Now Kara knew she had done her job well. Little Tang was happily making his way into the grown-up world.

 # Orangutan Facts

Orangutans live only in the lowland rainforests of Borneo and Sumatra in Indonesia. Their name means 'old man of the forest'.

Female orangutans are amongst the most caring, gentle mothers in the animal world. The males do not play any part in rearing their offspring.

A young orangutan will feed from its mother until it is about three and a half years old, and may stay with her until it is about eight. During this time it will learn all the skills needed to survive in the jungle, like how and when to find the best food, how to build a nest, and about parenthood.

Orangutans rarely go to the forest floor, where they may be in danger from tigers and wild boar. They spend their days high up in the trees, where they feed mostly on wild fruit. During the course of the day, they build several different nests from branches and leaves, where they will nap. Each night they build another nest.

Orangutans are endangered because large areas of the rainforest have been destroyed, leaving them with a diminished source of food.

For more information about Orangutans you can contact:
The Orangutan Foundation
7 Kent Terrace
London NW1 4RP